To children of all ages who celebrate autumn
with a visit to the pumpkin patch.

PUMPKIN HEADS!

Wendell Minor

iↄi Charlesbridge

October is here.
It's time to pick a pumpkin!

On Halloween, every pumpkin becomes a pumpkin head.

Some are **big.**
Some are small.

Some may float
high in the sky.

Some peek from windows.

And some go for a hayride.

A pumpkin head might pretend to be a cowboy . . .

or a snowman . . .

or a witch!

Some pumpkin heads
greet trick-or-treaters!

And some scare crows.

Pumpkin heads can be found in the strangest places.

But no matter where you find them, pumpkin heads of all shapes and sizes . . .

wish you a
Happy
Halloween!

Published by Charlesbridge
9 Galen Street
Watertown, MA 02472
(617) 926-0329
www.charlesbridge.com

Library of Congress Cataloging-in-Publication Data
Names: Minor, Wendell, author, illustrator.
Title: Pumpkin heads / Wendell Minor.
Description: Watertown, MA: Charlesbridge, [2021] | Originally published: New York:
Blue Sky Press, 2000. | Summary: When Halloween comes around, pumpkins
are turned into pumpkin heads of different kinds and greet trick-or-treaters.
Identifiers: LCCN 2018031384 (print) | LCCN 2018032443 (ebook) | ISBN 9781580899352
(reinforced for library use) | ISBN 9781632897886 (ebook)
Subjects: LCSH: Halloween—Juvenile fiction. | Pumpkin—Juvenile fiction. | Jack-o-lanterns—
Juvenile fiction. | Picture books for children. | CYAC: Halloween—Fiction.
| Pumpkin—Fiction. | Jack-o-lanterns—Fiction. | LCGFT: Picture books.
Classification: LCC PZ7.M669 Pu 2021 (print) | LCC PZ7.M669 (ebook) |
DDC 813.54 [E]—dc23
LC record available at https://lccn.loc.gov/2018031384
LC ebook record available at https://lccn.loc.gov/201803244

Printed in China
(hc) 10 9 8 7 6 5 4 3 2 1

Illustrations done in Designer's Gouache watercolor on Strathmore 500 Bristol paper
Display type set in P22 Garamouche by P22 type foundry, Inc.
Text type set in Billy by David Buck/SparkyType
Color separations by Colourscan Print Co Pte Ltd, Singapore
Printed by 1010 Printing International Limited in Huizhou, Guangdong, China
Production supervision by Jennifer Most Delaney
Designed by Diane M. Earley